MW01609178

For my girls.
You are my greatest inspiration.
❤️❤️❤️

MTSM Publishing
Copyright © 2020 by Angel Tate

Printed in the United States of America.
First printing 2020
ISBN 978-0-9992314-6-3

EVERYONE KNOWS
TO
COVER THEIR TOES

BY

ANGEL TATE

I'D LIKE TO TELL A TALE TO YOU THAT I HEARD LATE LAST NIGHT.
THIS TALE THAT I TELL....

WILL SURELY GIVE YOU A

FRIGHT!!!

IT'S THE STORY OF A
"THINGY THING",
I DOUBT YOU'VE EVER
HEARD.
THOUGH IF YOU HAVE,
I BET YOU THOUGHT THE
STORY WAS ABSURD.

NOW,
LISTEN CLOSELY

TO EVERY WORD I SAY, FOR IF YOU DON'T I PROMISE YOU,

DUN

DUN

DUUUNN!!!

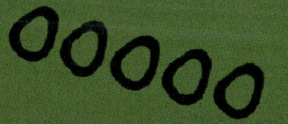

THERE'S A PRICE TO PAY

RUMOR HAS IT,
LITTLE EARL WENT
UPSTAIRS TO BED,
WITH HIS SUPERHERO
BLANKET AND A PILLOW
FOR HIS HEAD.

HE TOOK A FINAL SIP
FROM HIS FAVORITE
WATER CUP,

GRABBED HIS BLANKET BY BOTH HANDS AND PULLED THE COVERS UP.

IT WAS THEN,
I BELIEVE,
THE PROBLEMS
DID BEGIN. ALL
BECAUSE EARL
DIDN'T TUCK HIS
TOESIES IN.

HE DRIFTED OFF TO SLEEP. NO THOUGHTS OF THINGS THAT HIDE,

UNDER BEDS

IN
CLOSETS

WHERE THINGY
THINGS RESIDE.

BUT, TOES HAVE THAT SALTY SMELL THAT LETS A THINGY KNOW,
TONIGHT WILL BE THE NIGHT HE'LL GET TO FEAST ON TASTY TOE.

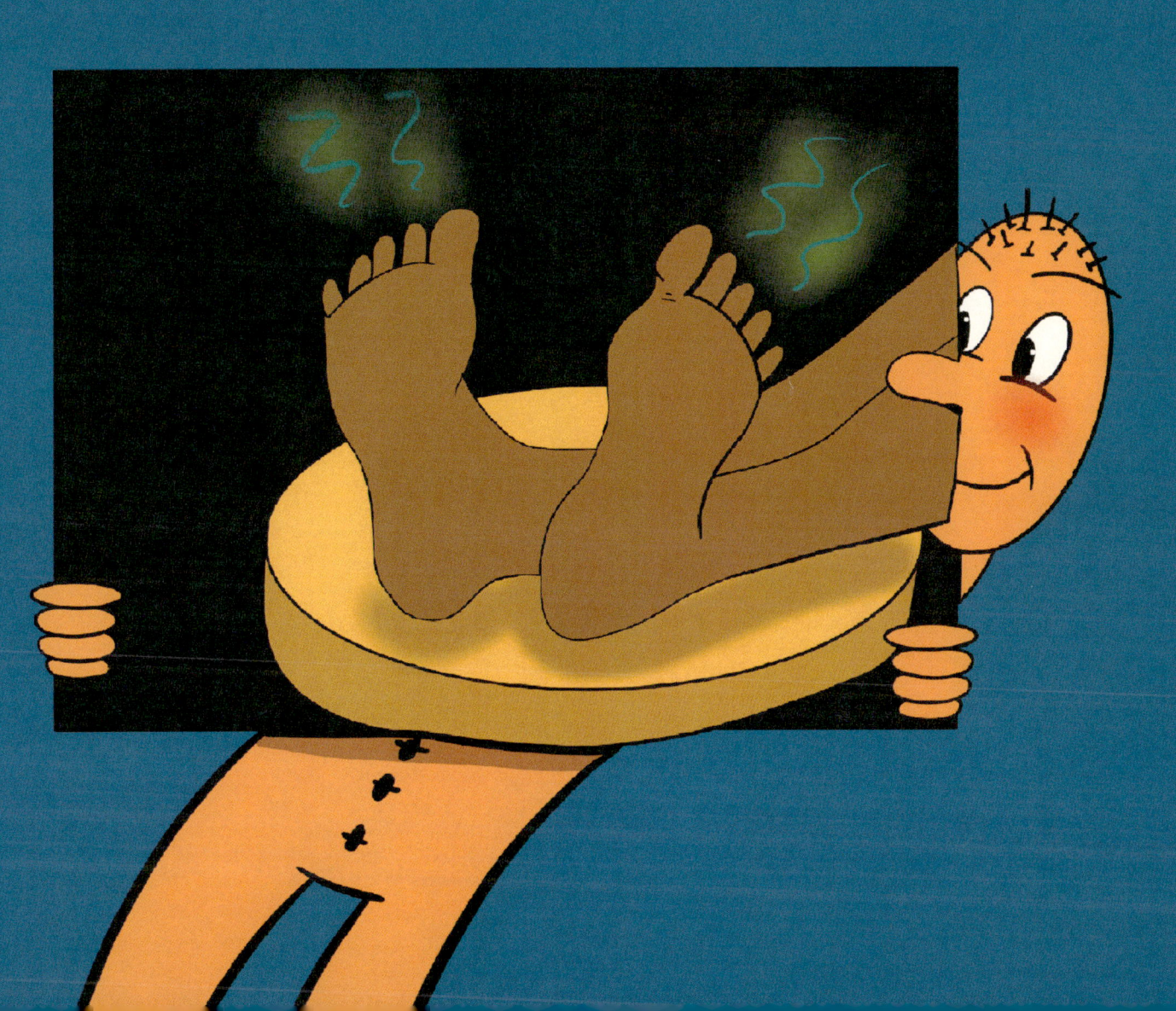

THINGY THING

LICKED HIS LIPS.
HIS EYE WAS BIG
AND ROUND.

SLIDING FROM BENEATH THE BED, HE DIDN'T MAKE A SOUND.

THINGY THING

LOOKED AROUND TO FIND UNCOVERED FEET.

HE WIPED HIS FACE AND HANDS IN PREPARATION FOR HIS TREAT.

TIP-TOE ACROSS THE FLOOR, THINGY THING MOVED IN. JUST BEFORE HE GOT A TASTE....

EARL

TUCKED

HIS

TOESIES

IN.

THINGY THING

DROPPED HIS HEAD,
SADNESS IN HIS FACE.
HE TURNED AND WENT
BENEATH THE BED,
BACK TO HIS **THINGY**
PLACE

NOW, LET THIS BE A
WARNING,
THIS SCARY TALE I
TELL.
READ THE STORY
MORE THAN ONCE
AND LEARN THE
MESSAGE
WELL.

YOU LEAVE YOUR TOES POKED OUT AT NIGHT.....

.... AND THEY
WILL COME
LICK YOU.

HEY ZION!
WHAT?
MOMMY SAID, STOP PLAYING WITH YOUR FRIENDS AND GO TO BED!
AWWW SHNUFFLEBUTT

THE

END

P.S. EVEN A THINGY
THING KNOWS TO
COVER THEIR TOES

Made in the USA
Columbia, SC
24 May 2021